Jackie Morris lives in a small house by the sea in Pembrokeshire, UK,
with children and dogs and cats. Ever since leaving college, Bath Academy of Art,
at least one cat has watched over her while she works,
sometimes helping with words, sometimes with the paintings.
Jackie's books for Frances Lincoln include *The Ice Bear*, *Tell Me a Dragon*,
and *The Snow Leopard*, winner of the Prix de l'Education Enfantine in France
and the Highland Book Award in the UK. She also illustrated James Mayhew's
Can You See a Little Bear?, Caroline Pitcher's *The Snow Whale, Marianna and the Merchild,
The Time of the Lion* and *Lord of the Forest*, and *How the Whale Became* by Ted Hughes.
The Seal Children was winner of the Tir Na N-og Award 2005.

www.jackiemorris.co.uk

For Thomas and Hannah and the Seals and Robin, with love

First published in Great Britain in 2004 by
Frances Lincoln Children's Books, 4 Torriano Mews, Torriano Avenue, London NW5 2RZ
www.franceslincoln.com

First paperback edition 2005

A catalogue record for this book is available from the British Library.

ISBN 978-1-84507-109-7

Set in Plantin

Printed in Heshan, Guangdong, China by Leo Paper Products Ltd. in June 2012

3 5 7 9 8 6 4

JACKIE MORRIS

The Seal Children

with best wishes
Jackie Morris

F

FRANCES LINCOLN
CHILDREN'S BOOKS

There is a place on the edge of Wales where fields and moorlands meet, where heather and gorse slope down to high cliffs. Waves crash and bite at the cliffs, and the wind lifts the spray as seals sing to the rhythm of the sea.

Stones and walls mark where a village once stood. There are no people now. All you can hear are the cries of buzzards, the chipping of stonechats, the tumbling notes of the skylarks and the distant song of the people of the sea.

Long ago, one of the sea people – a selkie –
came to live in the village. She fell in love
with the fair-faced, soft-voiced Huw who sang
as he fished. The people of the sea love music.

Surprised that such a love had come to him,
Huw welcomed the woman into his heart,
all the while knowing her for the wild creature
she was. As a sign of her love, she gave him
her salty sealskin to keep safe.

Time passed, and the sea-woman bore Huw twins with eyes
as sparkling and green as the waters of her home. The girl they
called Ffion, the boy Morlo – after the sea-woman's people.

The children helped their mother and father on land and sea.
Ffion fed the chickens, collected warm speckled eggs and planted
seeds in the garden. Morlo fished with his father, hauling nets
and crab-pots. The smell of the sea-salt was on his skin, and the
heather in his sister's hair.

In the evenings their mother sang them songs of life beneath
the sea. She told them of hills and valleys and weed-waving forests,
foam palaces and shining cities of gold and pearls.

How Morlo longed to see them!

Years passed, and the sea-woman began to change.
Her hair lost its shine, her eyes dimmed and
she found walking difficult. It was time for her
to go back.

Huw found her sealskin and one night, when
the summer moon was full and heavy, she walked
into the sea and plunged beneath the waves.
The water echoed with cries as the sea people
welcomed her home.

Huw turned and made his lonely way up
to his cottage.

From that day, his nets were always full.
The sea people guided shoals of sparkling fish
to his boat while Huw played tunes on his fiddle
to say thank-you.

One spring morning, a stranger came to the village.
In exchange for bread and fish and blackberry
wine, he told of his travels. And he spoke of a land
far away where people owned their own land –
where they profited from the fruits of their labour,
instead of watching the landlords cart away
the lion's share.

He stayed for a while, and a dream began
to form in the minds of the villagers. Now, all they
could think about was how to pay their passage
over the sea to the land far away.

So they searched their houses for farthings,
pennies and silver sixpences, for family treasures
to sell – until they realised that they would never
have enough.

But Ffion and Morlo remembered the stories
of palaces, sea people and cities of gold and pearls.

   The next full moon, they climbed down the steep
path to the stony beach. Everything was still and cold.
Together they sang a song to call their mother up
from her home.

   As the last note echoed in the dark caves, a sleek,
dark head broke through the water. Their mother
drew herself up from the water, beautiful and strong.
And as she hugged her children close, they told
her why they had come, asking, "Is it true? Are there
riches in your world? Can you help us?"

"Come with me," said their mother. "Come and see."

Morlo stepped forward eagerly, but Ffion drew back, unsure. The Selkie mother took her son's face gently in her hands and blew the salt breath of the sea three times into his mouth and nose. Then she led him down beneath the waves.

Fear gripped Morlo as they sank into the depths. Icy water cut through him and his lungs felt that they would burst from the shock as he gasped for breath.

Together they rose to the surface. He breathed again, and dived down with his mother – for they were two seals now. Down and down they went, to the hills, valleys and forests beneath the sea.

The light changed fast as streams of water stroked Morlo's face. Seaweed swayed in the strange currents and fish swam in and out of the forests like birds through trees. All around him his mother's people swam. And the sound of the sea rang in his ears as, far away, he heard the deep song of the great whales.

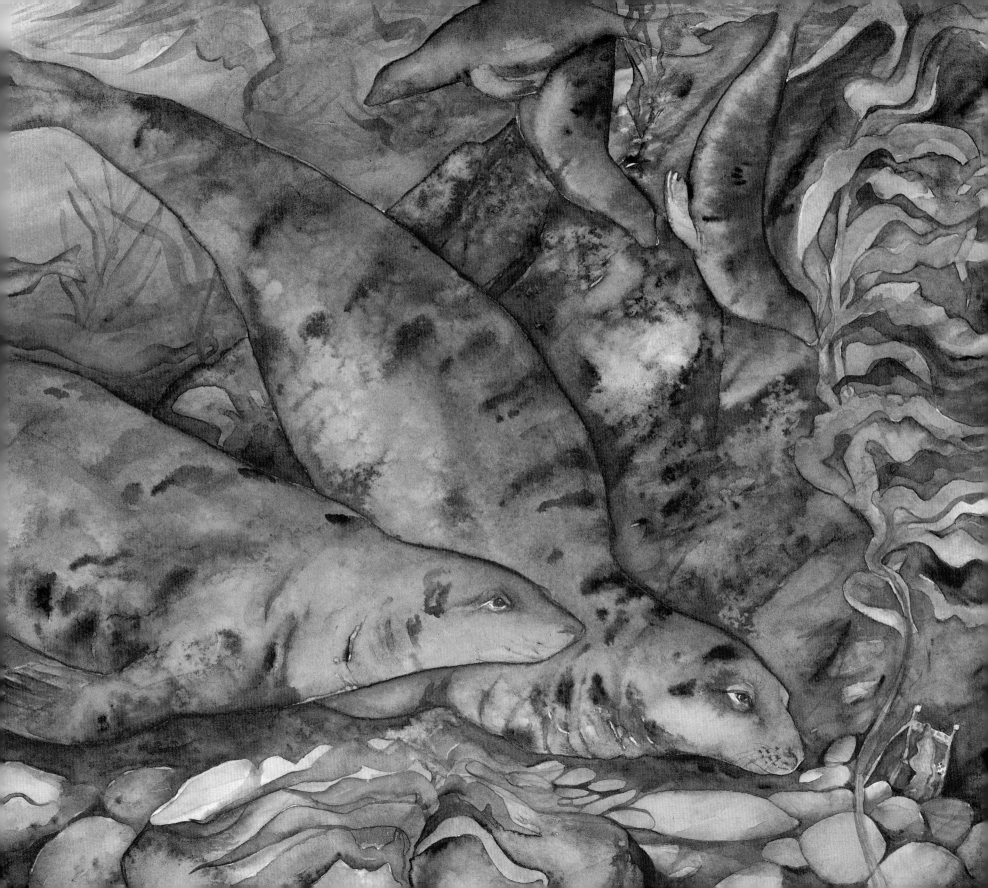

On the beach Ffion waited, fearful and shivering.

As the moon rose higher, she saw two sleek heads rise through the foam, and the moonlight glinted on a box tossed out of the waves at her feet. It was covered in barnacles and wrapped in golden ribbons of kelp.

Relief flooded through her as Morlo came out of the water. His eyes were full of excitement, and Ffion knew that he would return to the sea with his mother. They embraced and wiped salty tears from each other's eyes. Then once again the Selkie breathed the life of the sea into her son, and they slipped into the shining water.

Ffion climbed the steep path home, carrying the box.

Ffion found her father sitting by the fire. She pressed the box
into her father's hands. As they unwrapped the ribbons, she told
him of their meeting with their mother, of Morlo's journey beneath
the waves and of the joy in his eyes as he returned to the water.

They opened the box. Inside lay a heap of lustrous pearls.

The news spread quickly from cottage to cottage. The pearls
paid everyone's passage, and the villagers left their homes to sail
to the New World.

As they made their way down to the harbour, the village stood
empty behind them. Cats wandered in and out of the echoing
stone cottages; soon they, too, would be leaving in search
of new homes.

And as the ship carrying Huw, Ffion and the villagers
sailed out of Fishguard Harbour, two seals raised
their heads above the water and sang their goodbyes.

About the Story

Selkies or sea-fairies – half-human, half-seal – appear all around the British coast, and there are many stories about them. Usually they are women, but some are men. The legend goes that if you find the skin of a Selkie, you can keep her a prisoner on the land and she will become a faithful wife – but should she ever find her skin, she will return to the sea.

The village stands about a mile from where I live, perched above high cliffs. Called Maes y Mynydd *("Place of the Mountain"), it was inhabited until the beginning of the First World War. It is said that the people there became Quakers and wanted to go to Pennsylvania to start a new life, but they never raised enough money to go together and drifted off elsewhere. Life there was always hard, because all the cottages were tied to farms and even small children worked in the fields.*

There used to be a cove – now inaccessible – where the villagers kept fishing boats. Today the houses are ruined, but if you stand in the village in autumn, especially on a foggy day, you can hear the seals singing in the caverns below.

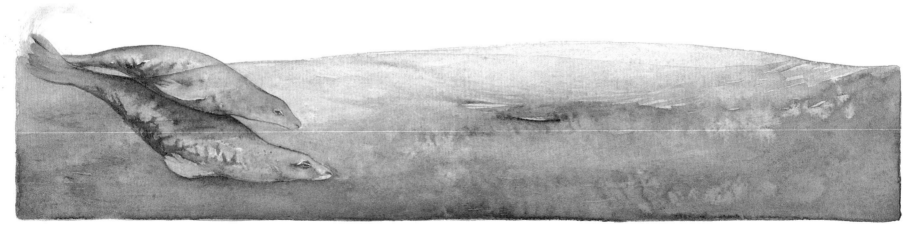

MORE TITLES BY JACKIE MORRIS
FROM FRANCES LINCOLN CHILDREN'S BOOKS

Lord of the Forest
Caroline Pitcher
Illustrated by Jackie Morris

For little Tiger, each new sound he hears in the forest
is exciting. But every time he tells his mother, she replies,
"When you don't hear them, my son, be ready. The Lord of
the Forest is here!" Tiger is puzzled, and as he grows bigger,
he asks all his friends – strutting Peacock, blundering
Rhino and trumpeting Elephant – to help him decide
Who is the Lord of the Forest?

The Snow Leopard
Jackie Morris

From the beginning of time Snow Leopard has sung
the stars to life, the sun to rise and the moon to wax
and wane. She weaves a song to keep her hidden valley
safe and as she sings, a child dreams her song. . .

The Time of the Lion
Caroline Pitcher
Illustrated by Jackie Morris

At night-time, when Joseph hears a Lion's roar, he decides
against his father's advice to go and meet the Lion. He
sleeps beside him, meets his brave lioness and watches the
cubs play, learning that danger is not always where you
think. Then one day traders come looking for lion cubs. . .

Frances Lincoln titles are available from all good bookshops.
You can also buy books and find out more about your favourite titles,
authors and illustrators on our website: www.franceslincoln.com